Ride to Live
Live to Ride

It's Not the
Destination...
It's the Journey

MARISA,

WE ARE SO HAPPY TO HAVE YOU AS
A GRAND DAUGHTER AND TO BE ABLE
TO WATCH YOU GROW INTO A STRONG,
SMART, CONFIDENT LITTLE GIRL.

MAY YOU TAKE THE TIME AND HAVE
FUN VISITING THE WONDERFUL PLACES
THIS COUNTRY HAS TO OFFER. AND
VISITING US TOO!

LOVE YOU
GRANDPA D&
MELINDA

This Book is Dedicated to the
Free Spirit and Child in all of Us.

Why Grandpa Rides a Harley

David Strange & Nancy Vogl
Illustrated by Nichoel Gibson

Cherry Tree Press
Traverse City, Michigan

Every summer Aidan visits his grandma and grandpa at their cottage on a lake. It's surrounded by tall pine trees and there are lots of things to do there.

Nearby are towering sand dunes to climb, lush forests to explore and endless beaches to play on. Aidan loves to go fishing and practice diving off the floating dock into the lake.

But more than anything, Aidan loves to help his grandpa tinker with his motorcycle. It's a bright blue, the color of the sky on a beautiful summer day. It has big fenders and the chrome is so shiny Aidan can see his reflection in it.

Aidan likes to run his hand up and down the black leather seat. Sometimes, if he's lucky, Grandpa even lets him sit on it for fun. When Aidan touches the handlebars, he pretends he's really riding it and he makes the sound of the bike... **Vrooom, vroooom!**

One morning while grandpa was polishing his motorcycle, Aidan sat down on the grass to watch him work. Suddenly curious, Aidan asked, "Grandpa, why do you love your motorcycle so much?"

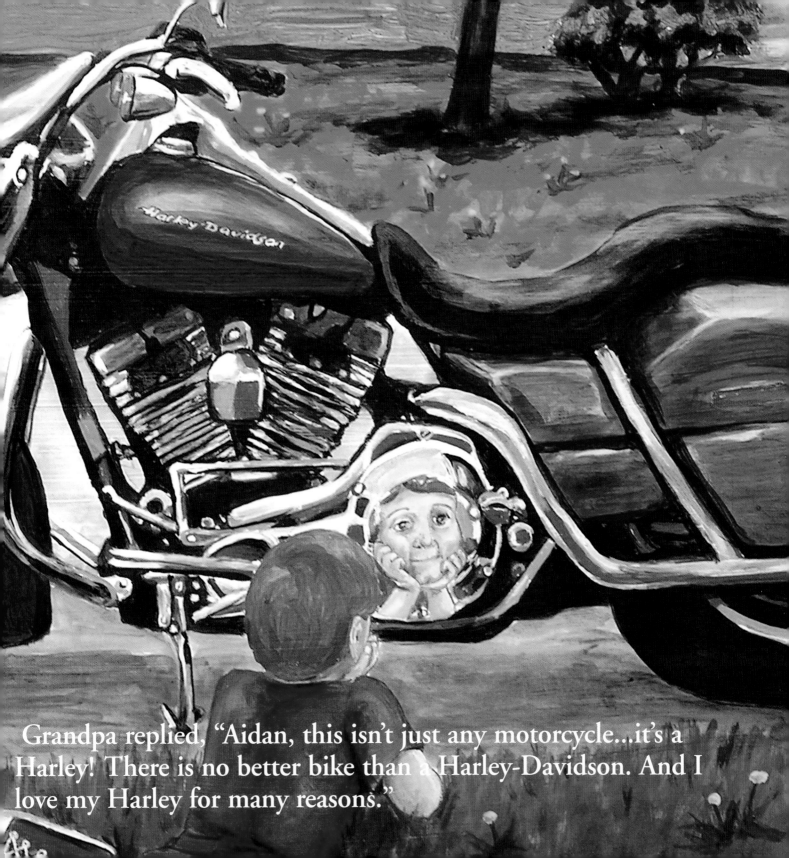

Grandpa replied, "Aidan, this isn't just any motorcycle...it's a Harley! There is no better bike than a Harley-Davidson. And I love my Harley for many reasons."

The name Harley-Davidson means it's the best motorcycle in the world and they have the coolest designs!

Some Harleys have bright colors and others have deep, dark shades. Some even have really fancy paintings on them.

But all Harleys are really beautiful. People turn their heads to watch whenever one goes by. They are so much fun!

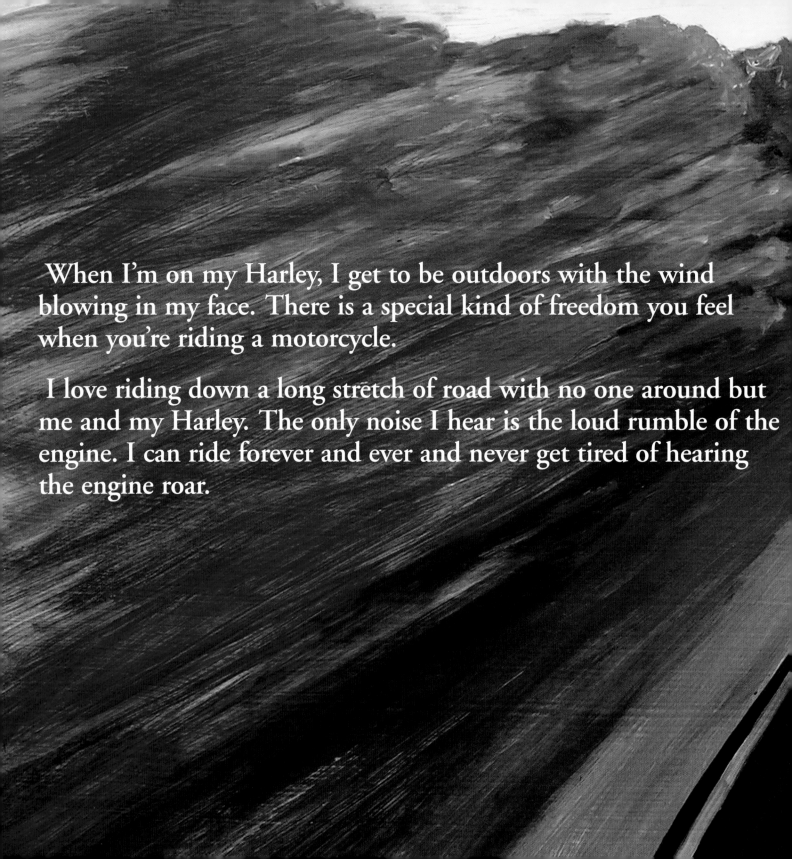

When I'm on my Harley, I get to be outdoors with the wind blowing in my face. There is a special kind of freedom you feel when you're riding a motorcycle.

I love riding down a long stretch of road with no one around but me and my Harley. The only noise I hear is the loud rumble of the engine. I can ride forever and ever and never get tired of hearing the engine roar.

And where I'm going isn't nearly as important as enjoying
the trip...kind of like how life is supposed to be.

Riding my motorcycle is a great adventure and there are so many things to see when you ride…I never get bored. I can go anywhere I want on my Harley!

I love to ride through farmlands and down quiet back roads.

I've ridden over magnificent bridges
and through great big cities.

I've seen gigantic mountains with snow dripping down them like melting ice cream. And it's an awesome sight to ride along the big, blue ocean with huge waves crashing on the shoreline.

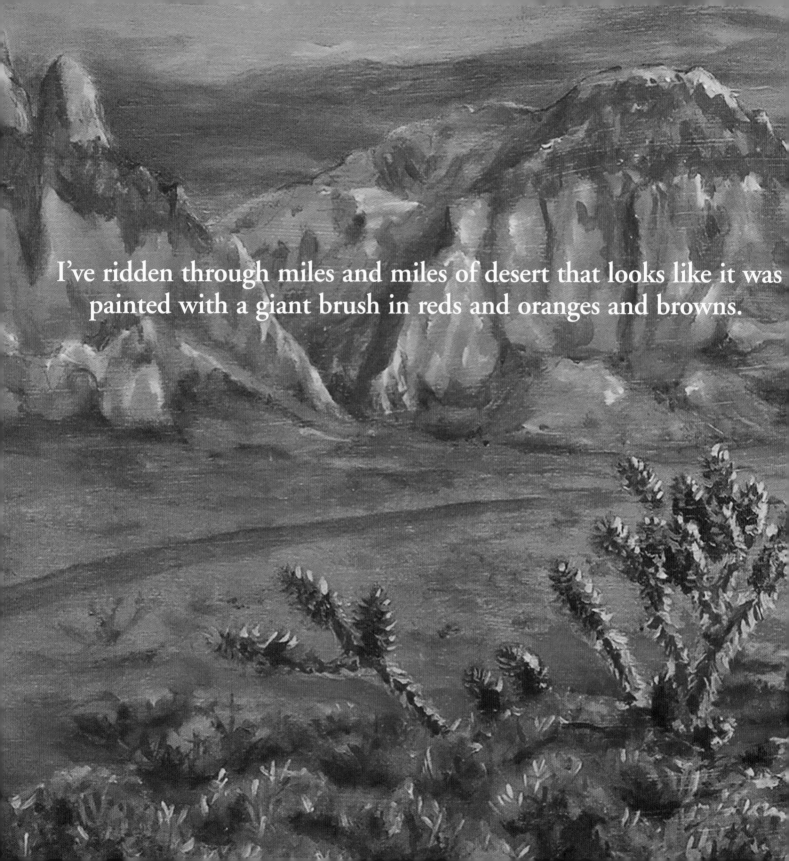

I've ridden through miles and miles of desert that looks like it was painted with a giant brush in reds and oranges and browns.

And I've seen the most spectacular sunsets when I've traveled on my Harley. The colors just burst across the horizon!

One of the best things about riding my motorcycle is meeting really great people and making lots of new friends. You're in a special kind of family when you ride a Harley. Some like to call it a "brotherhood."

All different kinds of people ride Harley motorcycles. Some are young, some are old. Some might work in a factory, or in a store. Some are teachers or doctors or moms who just love to ride.

Many of the people who ride Harleys like to get together at big events called a "rally." People come from all over the world to meet and have a good time. There is nothing like a Harley-Davidson rally!

When I'm on my Harley I have time to think about whatever I want to. I can dream big dreams and think wonderful thoughts. Some of my best ideas have come when I'm riding!

I get a peaceful feeling when I ride, almost like saying a prayer.
I forget about all my troubles and just enjoy my time.

Riding my Harley makes me happy and reminds me to be thankful for everything that is good in my life.

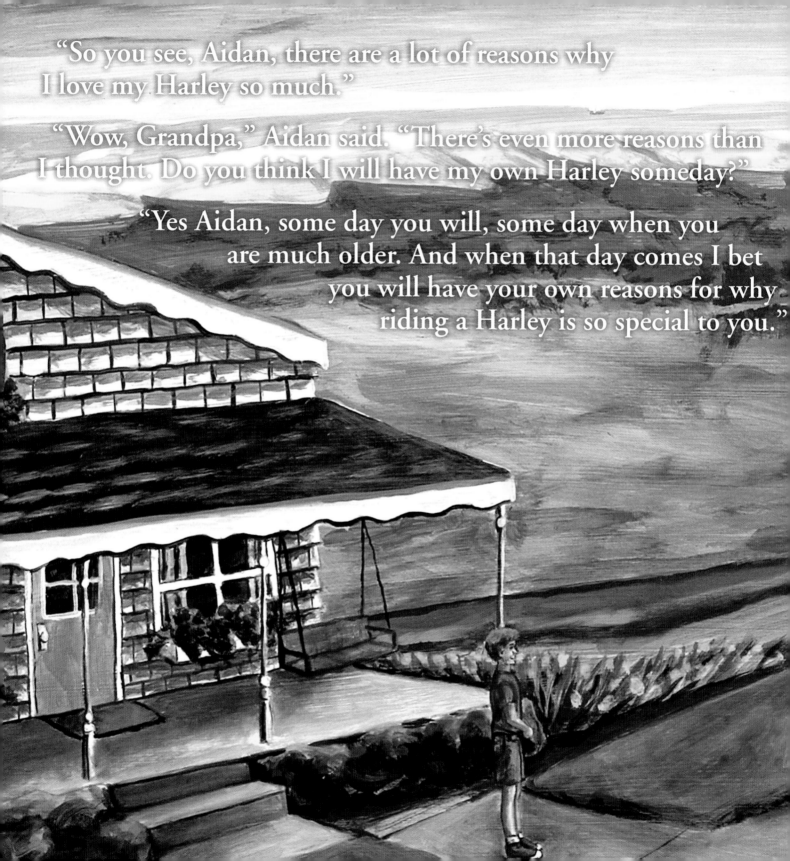

"So you see, Aidan, there are a lot of reasons why I love my Harley so much."

"Wow, Grandpa," Aidan said. "There's even more reasons than I thought. Do you think I will have my own Harley someday?"

"Yes Aidan, some day you will, some day when you are much older. And when that day comes I bet you will have your own reasons for why riding a Harley is so special to you."

Aidan became excited at the thought and headed back into the cottage. "Wait, Aidan," Grandpa said. "I forgot something really important to tell you. Do you want to know another reason why Grandpa loves to ride his Harley?"

"Yes, Grandpa, I do."

"Grandpa loves to ride his Harley...
because Grandma loves to ride her Harley too!"

If you would like additional copies of this book, please visit:
www.CherryTreePress.com
or inquire at your local Harley dealership

Ride to Live
Live to Ride
It's Not the
Destination...
It's the Journey